Autumn Leaves

By

Alfred Brock

Conversation and communication are gifts to us all. We can learn from each other. We can enjoy each other.

These poems and stories are collected from items written over a period of 40 years. Collected in the Autumn of 2022 they have been titled 'Autumn Leaves'.

Our individual perspectives in life and experience are all valid. They deserve to be shared.

What are yours?

Berries

Sweet Summer Berries
Morning light
Distilled

Work and exert
Till midday
When the berries are sweet

Water cold and wet

<u>Round the World!</u>

One clear tear

To dispel your fear

One full step

While you have wept

One bright cinder

As you call her

One gust of wind

To clear away sin

One cup of water

To mix in the lauter

One green bough

To place on the prow

One sweet berry

With which to make merry

One glad smile

To last for a while

Cast away, cast away, cast away now! We
sail to Jamaica and round the world!

<u>Rock Woman</u>

In the old days everything was dark
Rock Woman lay in the cold void

The one who made all, everything, saw this
and was sad
Rock Woman turned in the dark and sighed

She moved her foot and kicked a rock
It sparked
The one who made all, everything
Took the spark and blew upon it
The light grew and surged upwards
The one spark became many
The many became a shower
The void was filled with stars

Rock Woman sat up
She looked in wonder

Rock Woman gathered stones and rocks
near her
She fashioned them together
She smashed them together
She rolled them together

Rock Woman made the world

She placed the world around a star
The one who made all, everything
Saw this and was happy
Happy for Rock Woman as well

Time went on and Rock Woman made many
worlds
Set them to spinning around innumerable
stars

She became lonely
Rock Woman lay down among the worlds
Her feet, to warm them, she placed against
the stars

The one who made all, everything
Saw this and was concerned

Rock Woman, while in her sleep
Was placed down upon one of the rocky
worlds

She awoke in splendor at the dawn

But the earth was quiet

Rock Woman spun her hand and Wind
moved
At night the light from the sun was gone
To see in the dark
She pointed her finger at the sky
And poked a hole
There she placed the moon
It was not warm but she could read her
stories by

Wind was good and moved around but Wind
was dry
The Moon was good and lit the world but
the Moon was dry
Wind spoke to Moon
They could do nothing for her
Other than what they were
They waited

Rock Woman was thirsty
She lay down to sleep
Rock Woman dreamed the ocean

The ocean was filled with life

Violent and quiet from one moment to
another
Like Rock Woman
The sea was lonely
She shook out her skirts
Fish and birds fell into the waters
On the land the buffalo rose out of the
ground
The grass grew all around
The bears came out from the mountains
Ice melted and made rivers there

Rock Woman laughed
The rain came down from the sky

The one who made all, everything
Saw this and was glad

Glad for Rock Woman
Glad to have her as a helpmate

Rock Woman walks among the stars
Tending to all the planets and the people
To this day we can see her
When she passes

A long trail of fire and light rises up in her path
Cross the sky

<u>**Waiting**</u>

Eldon sat on a wooden chair next to a table piled high with magazines. In the center of the room there was another table with the Triangle Peg Game upon it. In the past that empty spot would have been filled with an ashtray but in these, the modern times, the Triangle Peg Game was there.

The rules of the Triangle Peg Game are simple. You must jump each peg over another peg, but only if there is an open space on the opposite side of the peg you are jumping. The object of the game is to remove all the pegs until one is standing. That is the popular idea of winning the game. The object of the game and eventual victory to Eldon was to remove all the pegs except the one and leave nothing but holes on the board.

He was very good at it.

He was so good at it that he won nearly every time he had played. In a strange way, it was the Triangle Peg Game that had given him the opportunity he had today.

His own father had always mocked him, asking, 'Do you want to end up digging holes your whole life?'

His father didn't appreciate his penchant for digging holes in the gardens, the backyard and around nearly every square yard on their property. Sometimes he was looking for buried treasure, sometimes he was helping his aunt to plant but most other times he was just digging holes.

He had come a long way in his life and his answer to his father's mockery became, 'Yes, I do want to dig holes my whole life!'

His gift had blossomed into opportunity and after nearly nine years of labor and after digging hundreds of thousands of holes here he was sitting in the outer office the Secretariat of Holes. He had visited so many offices and worked with so many clerks from the Hole Division to the Cleft Department and even once venturing into ditch digging but the length of the hole disturbed him. He liked it neat.

He worked most of those nine years for the same company. The Nominal Hole and Bore Company, LLC. The first four he was with them he was a Hole Technician. He worked hard and became a Hole Advisor.

By taking night courses he was able to master the art of Hole Design, Hole Extending and the Double Hole Bore. He graduate from the Hole Institute of

Margham, Michigan with top honors as a Hole Designer and Engineer.

He wanted to make his mark on the future of holes and so there he sat in the outer office of the Secretariat of Holes.

His mind, having wandered, snapped back to attention as the door opened and a man stepped forward towards him.

'Mr. Eldon DePression?', asked the man.

'Yes, that's me.', said Eldon.

'Follow me.', said the man beckoning to Eldon.

Eldon followed him into the great expanse and emptiness beyond the door and left the waiting room.

<u>Wise Ones Opine</u>

It was long time ago and away

These things that happened

That I am going to say

Along the shivering coast

Of the Great White Lake

That sits like a ghost

In the ice and mist

Of the Great North Woods

Gingerella was a fella' from way out yonder
somewhere

Beyond the place of ice and snow

A place from whence the winds do blow

Sitting there he pondered square

His duty to himself

He had to admit

There wasn't much to it

He had better get going somewhere

So he called the east wind

And caught him a ride

Upon the White Lake's beach

He wandered south

Filling up his eyes, his head and his mouth

With berries and fruits and nuts of winter

In frigid waters he pawed out icy treats

The mussels and clams and oysters to eat

When one day he came upon

A small little hamlet

Not much bigger than a settlement

But older than it should have been

It was here he was captured by the Pirates of
the North

And kept in a box until their captain came
forth

But wise was Gingerella and immune was
he

From the nasty pirate glances

Their taunts and pleas

One day while they were waiting he
convinced them all then

To let him out a bit to walk among men

They laughed and they joked

They stuck and they poked

And when he suggested

They were all just cowards

They flung open the door

And so

Commenced their final hours

Gingerella laughed and he danced

He told wondrous stories of genies and
lamps

He gave forth the impression it had all
happened to him

And I, for one, can tell you, it is so, I will
not grin

He bellowed and pranced and yanked and
guffawed

He yanked and he took and talked them all
raw

Finally he gained their respect and their awe

They thought to themselves

With him on our side

We would always win

Take it all in stride

They showed him their treasure

He laughed deep inside

He reached out to take

They warned him aside

'The Captain is Coming! Leave it all as it
is!'

Gingerella thought a moment and pointed to
the sky

See there the stars boys? They are all in
your eyes.

But here on the beach

Within easy reach

Are all the treasures you need

Fought for and pinched!

It's here now, boys! It belongs all to you
all!

Says I, Gingerella, let no captain stall!

Says they to him the Captain is weird

He frightful and angry and greedy and slim

He'll chop off your head with a big toothy
grin

He'll put cheese on it then and dip it in gin

He's not to be trifled with

This large Captain Grim

Gingerella just laughed and cared not a wit

He gathered the gold and jewels in his mitt

He stuffed them all that he could

In his bright shiny beard

He told them they should too

Then listen and hear

What he would do

When the Captain came near

Wait long they did not

The Captain returned right there on the spot

Gingerella he met with a nod and a glance

Gingerella returned with a capstan and lance

He placed them all on it

Round then he spun them

Till the Captain and crew

Had all come undone

Then with jewels and with gold

Stored safely in beard

Old Gingerella laughed and cried out

'They thought the Captain was weird.'

Gingerella walks

Where they bears they do not

He flies on the air

In cold, dreadful draughts

He knows of no fear and looks for a good
time

It's wise to stay wide of him

Wise ones opine

Tomorrow

See the wall

It is so flat

It hurts my back

To lie down

On this cold, hard floor

But I'll be happy

'Cause tomorrow

I'll be married

To you

In a little church

On the little hill

Outside of town

We'll be happy

Leave the Trees

Blue Wood

Painted Wood

Let them stand

They're much prettier

Tall and green

In the forest

Not to eat on

To save them

Leave them

1.4.79

<u>**All Night**</u>

Fresh water

Fresh Coffee

What I need

Fresh Coffee

I've been up all night

1.4.79

Cold Water

Water cold as ice

Real nice

To swim

A whim

The river

The water

Cold, cold water

1.4.79

<u>Home</u>

Home

Could I come home

Wanting to come home

Can I

Please

Come home

I pray

To come home

I'm coming

Wanting to be home

I'm coming

Home

There at home

Home, Home, Home, Home

1.4.79

Living Beauty

What is living

   Breathing

What is living

   Running

What is living

   Walking

What is living

   Seeing

What is living

   Wanting

Living is Friends

1.4.79

<u>Double Gladness</u>

Could it be

One day

     A letter fell onto the ground

And grew

Carrying news

     From love and kindness

Into a building

To a man

     Standing tall

Containing love and riches

Who strayed

    From the home

To the son

The letter

    He went

1.4.79

<u>Abstract Evening</u>

Changes were made

In the heat

    In the night

New pieces laid

In the heat

    In the night

New morning haze

Comes with early light

    Flowers all ablaze

From

The heat

In the night

1.4.79

Communicating

She sat in the kitchen.

The light from the early morning sun streamed in through the window. Passing through the red checkered curtain the sun's indirect rays splashed upon the tabletop before her.

The top was formica colored as white marble with gold streaks running through it. She had always liked the table. When she and her husband had brought the table home she was satisfied with it. It was a couple of weeks, however, before the sun was high enough in the sky to paint the light picture on the table's surface that she had become so enamored of.

She leaned back. It took a while she recalled. For the light to come in. Then another little while to become used to it.

They had the table for two years. She reflected on how she felt as the sun changed direction in the sky and the way the light fell upon the table in the morning changed. She found herself waiting for Spring and Summer to come on again so that she could enjoy the light on the table again.

'Such a small thing.', she thought to herself. She stood up and moved some dishes around in the sink. Her husband would be down soon. She nervously puttered about. The last eight days had been extremely stressful for her. His drinking had caused her nervousness. As it progressed and he became morose and threatening at time she began to fear his drinking. She would take herself away from him.

She would isolate herself in the house and avoid him. She began to spend a lot of time sitting at the kitchen table in the evening. At first, sitting nervously, then, later, she began to move some of her things into the kitchen. She would read at the table. Prepare and eat her food at the table. Slowly she began to not call friends on the telephone in the evening. As she shut down communication they also did and the calls coming in were reduced. She sat down again. With dish towel in hands she twisted it slowly in her hands. She wrenched at it and clutched it to her face as she recalled that humiliating call with her closest friend and he had come storming into the kitchen.

He was loud and obnoxious, bullying and nearly incomprehensible. He was loudly abrasive as he demanded to know where the rest of his beer had gone. 'There's none in the refrigerator!', he thundered. 'Where did it go? Where did it go? Did you take it?' She tried to address him but his shouting grew ever louder. He had startled her so that it wasn't for a few minutes until she remembered she had been talking on the phone. She returned to the call for a moment and said, 'Something's come up. I'll have to say good-bye now.' Then the rest of that night had gone on into a shouting nightmare.

Finally, against her protestations, he took himself out of the house and drove in a drunken fit to the store to buy more beer. She put the cloth back in her lap, still clutching it with both hands. He must have calmed down by the time he had arrived at the store or they wouldn't have sold him more. She had hoped he had been kicked out of the store. She knew, however, that even if he appeared in that particular convenience store, known jokingly as a Party Store, that they would welcome him with open arms as long as he opened his wallet and paid them their money.

She had seen them haul cases of beer out to pickup truck that belonged to the old man living down the road. She had a terrific fear that her husband would one day turn into that. A shell of man maintained by the constant imbibing of alcoholic beverages. Her husband had already started to lose the command of speech. Wildly ranting the same phrases over and over. At first he had sought her out to abuse her verbally but the last year he had stopped doing that. He stayed to himself.

After drinking a while he would start mumbling and then move on to speaking aloud. While talking to himself on and off he would escalate into shouting matches with unseen foes. His opponents always seemed to be so much more powerful than him. After some fits of rage had gone by he would be reduced to mumbling again, and then, finally, pass out. Oblivious to the world, himself and to her. The Party Store.

She had used to be a regular customer there. Stopping in to buy the newspaper or milk or some occasional pastry item. She had stopped going there after one ugly incident with her husband. She had stopped in for something, she couldn't recall what, and he had been there. He was particularly drunk.

She instinctively tried to avoid him but either her swift motion or the sound of the clanging bell that hung above the door caught his attention and he turned. He began to shout at her. Asking why she was hiding. Accusing her of following him. He berated her while the store clerk stood idly by staring and watching the whole ugly incident. A young boy at the back of the store popped his head out from around one of the aisles and simply said, 'Hey, Mister!', in a plaintive voice. It was enough to turn his head and she took the opportunity to slip out the door. She hadn't set foot in the place since then.

One thing she clearly remembered from that day was the advertisement next to the stack of her husband's favorite beer. It showed a large group of people clustered around a grill cooking food. Behind them was a semicircle of powerful pickup trucks and fancy cars. All of them had beers in their hands or near them. She thought, 'Is that an advertisement for drinking and driving?' They were on a beach. The sun was shining.

The light from the sun was emphasized as it streamed down from the sun in the photograph. She remembered thinking it was so fake. So fake. Not like the sunlight on her table at all. She went home. As she sat staring down at the cloth she was clutching she became aware of the light flowing into the rest of the kitchen, illuminating it at each corner.

She looked up to her display of cooking spoons hung on the wall over the table. They gleamed silver in that bright golden light that was pouring now like a flood into the kitchen. She heard the first stirrings from upstairs.

He was awake.

She had taken to sleeping in her sewing room. She had set up the sofa in there into a comfortable bed and had slowly begun to move all of her personal belongings in there. He had asked her on a couple of occasions why she was sleeping in there. She had given him a rather detailed explanation at one point but it became apparent he was not only not paying attention but that he was so drunk he was incapable of understanding what she was saying. That was when she had begun to fear him when he was drinking.

Time had passed and her new normal was a lonely life, punctuated by an odd call from her lifelong best friend. The woman tried to reach out but she, attempting to safeguard her friend, only succeeded in pushing away the one bridge to freedom she might have been able to take.

So it went on. Day after day. Week after week. Month after month.

Now, three years later, something was changing again. She heard his footsteps on the stairs. He moved down them cautiously but with intent. He went outside to pick up the newspaper and returned. She heard him just on the other side of the wall as he placed it on the dining room table. In a moment his face would appear from around the doorframe that connected the kitchen to the dining room.

She sat rigidly erect. Her hands again clutching the faded cloth. The light shone down on her shoulders. Even though it was still chilly and damp outside at this time in the morning at this time of the year she could feel the warmth of the sun upon her back. Like the gently pressing of a friendly hand the sun was at her back. His head appeared around the doorframe. 'Good morning to you.' 'Good morning.', she said.

He stepped into the kitchen and took down a coffee cup. He filled it up with the black stuff. Stepping over to the refrigerator he opened it in a jerking fashion as he always had done. He reached in and took out the milk carton. He looked at it for a moment, then, over at the cup of steaming, black coffee. He shook his head and returned the carton into the refrigerator and closed the door.

He turned to glance at her. Momentarily. His lips curled into a gentle smile. Only at the corners of his mouth, indicating that he was happy, in a good mood and at peace with the

world. 'If only this could last.', she thought.
He picked up his coffee and left the room.
He called out as he exited the front door,
'See you later!'

Sitting on the edge of her seat she did not
respond. The door closed and he was gone.
A tear slid down her face from her right eye.
She gently moved the cloth in her hands to
wipe it away. 'If only this could last.', she
said aloud. 'How long will this last?'

It had been eight days since his last drink. It
hadn't even registered with her at first. It
took a couple of days before she noticed that
his ranting had ceased. It took a few days to
understand that she was hearing silence
when she had previously heard banging and
muttering and shouting.

Eight days. 'How much longer will this
last?'

She knew she didn't know. She also knew in her heart that if she didn't seize these moments right now they may never return.

Even in the face of the fear of its returning – all that cacophony and danger and uncertainty – she knew she had to do something. What? She stood up and stepped slowly around the table to where the wall phone hung. She took up the handset and began to dial. The sun was positioned so now that the sunlight streamed through the window and into her eyes.

'So much light!', she thought. She briefly covered her eyes with the towel in her hand and then, lowering it, gazed out into the yard and the fields beyond. The sun warmed her. On the other end of the line the phone began to ring.

<u>**Shhhh!**</u>　　　　July 2, 1982

The Cougar moves, a bolt of light

Colored tan

Glowing blue in the night

Snow plays mirror with the moon

Sky electrically charged

Coug

Claws of Stars

Flashing hot sparks

Extended, retracted

Mighty tail swinging

Whipping strange serpentine arcs

Body

Standing poised

Ears

Listening

Wind singing to it

Of ice and windswept snow banks

A hare?

Has the wind borne knowledge of the

Creature where it was? Is?

No matter

Cougar moves on

Slinking

Padding

Barely audible crunch

On snow's unbroken and uneven surface

Paws padding o'er the silken snow floating
suspended

Above the earth

Moving

Transparent

Snow envelopes the cougar's presence

Filling the space of its passing

Beyond

Snow glimmers placidly

Uncaringly

Moon smiles unceasingly

On its child

Yellow Ghost

Wandering bolt of light and life

Packed with death

To energize its life

Cunning

Violent

Beautiful in awesome power

Adventuresome freedom

Killing for freedom

Nourishment, Fear, Power

Cougar being

Unto itself

Drawn from the life around it

Woe to the human

Standing before it

Unless of proper courage and power

Wild as the cat itself

So now

So now

It's gone

Padding restlessly

Ceaselessly

Quietly gone

Shhhh!

<u>It's a ha ha</u>   July 2, 1982

City fills up

Quiet

You can feel it

Yet not see it

Like an oxen's tail

Swatting at a fly

Feeling

Reaction

All around

Other oxen

Indifference settles

Or a smile

This is command

This is gazing out

Two others sharing this rock

Is this not like earth

Up

Down

Out

In

Conversation

Creation

So it does

So it goes

"Words are just words."

Are they?

Communication

Some say something

Some say nothing

We command understanding

We command life

Bodies like fire

Flickering

Words like embers

Swirling in smoke

Mixing together

Spreading

Fire

<u>**As You Are**</u>   July 2, 1982

Do as you are

As you feel

As you be

As you are

Life gives

What you give

To others to see

Be as you are

As you feel

As you be

As you are

A smile is worth it all

Thoughts up in the wind

All the same

When a smile

Casts its gold

Be as you are

As you fee

As you be

As you are

Take away the pain

Live like a raindrop

Slowly falling

Glistening

In the wind

Be as you are

As you feel

As you be

As you are

Rain will rise up

From the land

To clouds

Into life again

Green and verdant

Cloak of earth

Sweet coat plant

Be as you are

As you feel

As you be

As you are

<u>So Does He</u>   July 2, 1982

Blind one

Watches us go by

Can you help me?

Goes the plaintive cry

Cannot use my eyes

Life

Takes me where it will

What I know and have known and will know

Taken

From a world invisible to me

Life

Has been kind

Trusting as I am

I see evil

Casting no demeaning glances then

Life has taught me

To love

Take chances

Sing out loud

To the crowd

Life has been to me

Even though I cannot see

I feel love

In strangest places

I know happiness

In friendly faces

I know

Do you?

I am close to God

He holds me in His bosom

Caresses my weary head

Blesses me again

Sends me on my way

To let you all know

Today is the day

Life has been good to me

Life is being good to me

I will be good to you

I love you and so does He

<u>Eyes Behind Sunglasses</u>   July 2, 1982

Differences

Educations

Abound

Perceive

Pretty

Nice

Brown hair

Eyes behind sunglasses

Holds You Up

July 2, 1982

Back to the flowers

Dearest children

Mind

Crystal light of stars

Reach and hold

Be held

Behold

Our hearts are one

Like a flower

Divine diversity knows no bounds

We grow up and out

Let us be steadfast and loyal

Let our branches intertwine

Fear not

To stand out

We grow tall together

Forever

We who are one

Are strong

Follow and lead

It is the way

Be in your way

Hanging suspended

The world holds you up

Out of the world

We are, yes

<u>Joy and Living</u>   July 2, 1982

From the Barker's call of "ishe! – ishe!"

To the flags flapping in the wind

This is New York

In the beginning

Of the seventh month

This year

One thousand, nine hundred

Eighty two

A sizable number

But we remember

Twice times thrice

Times twice again

Times what time is

More than that

In clarity

For we look out now

We remember the stars

The Moon

The Sun

Have always been here

As we have

Waiting

For our time

And now that it is here

We spend it reveling

Touching one another's lives

Living growing

Outward upward

Tis true we are not alone

For all around us we keep ourselves

Seemingly quite alone

But it's nice to have a friend

Tis true I will not desert a true friend

Nor them I

But a moving away will do

If he presence becomes too stifling

And we need freedom

But again we will come together

For we always need freedom

Live well and gather what you can

It is all not for naught but for

Joy and Living

Package in Hand   July 2, 1982

Mr. Randall

Please excuse my pettiness

Of course

You had packages in hand

Sorry

A word not quite correct

I wish you well

In your deeds

With a hope that more civil

Manners will remain in me

For I have better

I have done better

Not lesser

May your day be good

The light shine upon your face

And you works

To remain

This is a pitiable semblance of

An appreciative piece to the monument

Of a man

So that is that

I'll Never Leave Her   July 2, 1982

You came into my life

Now I'm changed forever

Yes again

This world is so beautiful

I don't see it

Unless I see you

You give wings to my soul

Lift up with me

This glorious being

Stars on her wings

Flying with me

Sacred woman

Life

Way

This is it, oh!

I'll never leave her

<u>Tree Before Me</u>   July 2, 1982

Excalibur

Steel of excellence

Excalibur

Make a Knight from a Boy

King from a Knight

Piece so glorious

Sun shines through it

Best held

Gripped by a King

Fate decided

Forged at the beginning of Time

Display of power in unity

To the world

Forged by no mortal man

Yet to be

This tree before me

Yet to be

This mind in me

When revealed

To stand beside her then

Yet to be

Now is

<u>Alive</u>   July 3, 1982

Tell me

This is Supernatural Power

Do it!

Don't!

Ramifications of a bit of a look

Caught on my face

By another's eyes

Till my voice

Rings silent

Choked with emotion

Deluge begins

Changing my mind

As my tongue these worlds entwine

I let it happen

So there's nothing more to do

Nothing

To complain about

I will so

As I am about to do

Alive

<u>Off To Sleep</u>   July 6, 1982

I hear

Ancient highway

Rolling Underneath wheels

Night blacker

Than any city in slumber

Stars sparkle bright

Painting shapes dreamt

By those whose meanings read

Of life in sweeping arcs of suns

While scent of evergreens

Fill my nostrils

Yet again

Expanded out under the dome of night's sky

What glanced that?

Caught in briefest beam of light

Golden Stage or Silver Hare?

Gone in comet flash

Too dark to track

Return then back

To head back

Sit then archer

In the black

Await the bear

On hidden track

Twins are by

In sleep enfolded

Their power waits the morning Sun

Their Father

Walks tomorrow's light tonight

<u>Three Rabbits</u>   July 6, 1982

Three Rabbits

Two Jacks and a Doe

Dancing in the grass

Racing through the evening

With a mindful thought

As they consume their clover

Whoo and they run

Hopping through the grass

The doe nibbling gently

Who will she stay with?

One chases other through the stands of grass

So much younger

So much stronger

Running him down

Running him up

What if he falls?

Racing

Rabbits on

Time to leave

They have nothing to do with me anyway

<u>If I'd Only</u>   July 7, 1982

I'd rather

Live with the wind in my hair

Than to sit alone

And not remember where

My keys are

I'd rather learn

How to travel far

Than to sit alone

In this bar

For long

I'd rather be

Where the wind takes me

Across the horizon

Far out to sea

Than to think

There's nowhere to be

I'd rather let

My heart out to the stars

Than to sit among people

Who stare at cars

Wondering, why me?

Thinking I'm coming home

Then to sit in a house

And know I'm not there

But where?

Is your smile and your laugh?

Where is the baby daughter who would grab
at your calf?

You left us

In a brief lullaby

Gazing at each other asking, 'Hey! Why?'

This is a life

To have and to hold

But you blew it all

By being so bold

I'd rather be free

On the road

In the night

Than to work at a job

That hides all the light

I'd rather be

Alone and aflame

Than sitting and piddling

In some little game

I'd rather

Hear the storm

Blow through and grind

Than to curse the destroyed

Pretend they're not mine

I'd rather race in the air

Against an unsure feeling

Than to fester somewhere

With my eyes on the ceiling

Knowing that I could have been right

If I'd only…

<u>Lost Bound</u>   1982

Ground

Into

Shaky pavement

Some things

Flying around, viewed

Someone lost

People talking, scrounging, pointing, losing,
winning, indicating, all around

Some lost

What is going on there?

What is?

Everything comes crushing in

Someone lost

Someone is lost

Hope to break through fresh light

Does not seem possible

Now

Night sky black

Star sprinkled

People miss

One another

Lost

They might be here, missed

So much, missed

So much lost

Another one

Heads for the edge

No one knows

They're only going

Until they're gone

Lost

Some

No one knows

When everyone is lost

Let's just be happy and

Be happy

<u>Red Blood</u>   July 7, 1982

I need to feel

The wind on my face

My red blood

Racing

In a strange, new place

Where squirrels

Aren't sitting

Fat Bread and Scared

I want to be

Where my teeth can be bared

I long to be

Where I can be understood

Where my rightful place

Is all well and good

I want to walk

Where the wind

Is wild and free

I want to be

Where the birds

Will talk

To me

<u>**Not Finished Yet**</u>   July 7, 1982

You took your life in your hands

You sent it up in flames and glory

Who is to say

That life

Didn't take you?

Like a ripe banana falling to earth

Ripe seed bursting out its pod

Vine wrapping to the ground

Up again growing

Entwining a tree

Encircling

Pulling down

To destruction

Where is your life now?

Spiritual tree

How has it been taken from you?

With steel and fire?

With crushing force?

With annual weight and closing in?

You

Out of sight

Ducking behind the moon

Flung from ruddy, red, foggy earth

To dark night and shadow

You attempt

To hide your face from the Sun

Yet, even, the moon, in vacuum space

Shows all parts to

That celestial light blooming

Come round again

Gleaming

Towards down

Dark red

Shining

Bursting back

Into the sun

When we look again

The moon is still there

You here

<u>We Remember</u>   July, 1982

Little piece missing

All there

Next night

One bit hidden

Not by the earth

By shadow bent

Sun shines on, bright and powerful

While dawn races round the earth

Night beyond

Sun newly minted

Takes our breath away

Morning breeze to cool our brows

Leave us cool from night night's heat

Fire in our bellies

Warmth within our hearts

Words, songs and actions

Fill our days with varied parts

Behind you

Left a singing note

You are the string

Bent

Released

Then sounding

Reverberating

Echoing

Changing the changeless within

Sound expanding

Again a new singing

Song on song singing

Soul

Being

Silence then

Left like the sting of a bee

Is the flier gone?

The stinger remains

Remained

Gone

The song erupts

New

Promise of future ignited

Sun within my hands

Sound in my ears

Like light

In my eyes

Away

I shed tears

In my joy

Away

I witness

The sound of the spheres

How is it

That?

You can speak this language

Make the planets ring

Revolve around the stars

While I

In mute appreciation stand

Close by

Your warmth and light

We remember you

We remember

<u>Wonder Why</u>   July 1982

It doesn't

Take too much

To see past the sky

In darkest night

Blue shade drawn

Clouds apart

Stars of time revealed

I wonder

Who else is looking

Wonder

Why

<u>Eagle</u>   July 12, 1982

This Wind

Beginning at the tip of Manhattan

Flowing through

The hundreds

Catching on Fifth Avenue

Ripping down it

Only to find

An eddy

In the green eye

Central Park

Where

Children playing

Gaze

Upon an eagle

<u>Away to Sea</u>   July 1982

Devourer of song

Minion of the Sky

Longing to sail on

With net on knees

Mending

Eyes upon the waves

No obstructions

Just command

Might torrent of wind

On water

Sprayed

Wiping eyes

Clearing face

Tanned

Brown

Slowly turning storm

Goes out to sea

<u>Keep the Flow</u>   July 13, 1982

Keep the Flow

The fire burning

Fill up your heart

Spirit you away

Thence

So

Keep the Flow

The fire burning

Keep the Flow

<u>**Wait**</u>   July 1982

Look!

I have made a wall around you

I have made a dream real

Look

The wall before you

Turn to run away and you run into it

Run back

Again you face the barrier

To the sides?

Yes

As you rise

To clamber over

The wall rises

To meet you

So

Go down

It sinks to lowest point

To meet you

Look

All in a bundle

What you have

Who you are

Feel this wall

Face to face

Close

See through it

Transparent

Be throught it

But

Cannot

See the outside then

Lift your senses

Lift your eyes

Lift your heart

I have a built a wall

You strive to cross it

Over

Under

Around

Through

The Barrier

Never seeing

That you are not the one

So

Confined

<u>**Key**</u>

He stepped

Into the night

Mist

All around

Filling his nostrils

With wet odors felt

Rushed down within

Lungs awash in evening moisture

Night's clammy touch

The wetness

Caught him

Off guard

As if someone

Had grabbed his garment

He stumbled

Eyes widening

Head thrown back

Gasping

Watching

Fog coming down

First, second, third

Trailing wisp of mist

Leading the fog

To him

Sliding the fog

To him

As he watched

Silken cord of smoke

Closed about him

Until his eyes

Adjusted

To the fuzzy light

He shuddered

Found his front door key

<u>Infinite</u>

I can see

Very far back

In the blue

Of this television

Screen

The blue

Program

Blue

Of Forever

Indulging

We can see

Infinitely

Whenever

We gaze

Or think

Then

We

Are infinite

Awakening

Awakening

From deep

Refreshing

Sleep

Stretching

Before

The Rising Sun

Like ancient

Oblation

My body

Offered

What Star is this?

Comes next thought

So many, many

Before

Wind

So kind

In dune depression

Roars

Above my head

Now again

Grasped

In gravity

Held

The sands around me

Shifting

Slowly

Hidden ocean

Beyond just bare horizon there

So closely perceive

After

Distanceless voyage

Of blue or green or blackened waters

I cannot tell

This morning new

Lifting from my face

I smell the air

Fresh ocean breeze realized

<u>Varied Forest of Your Life</u>

It is true

All women should have

A poem written for them

It is also true

Some deserve volumes

You are of those

My love

There is, however, not enough time for that

 I then, must, fill this time with deeds and actions

The better for you

To see and feel and hear and know

 While in the night, during your slumbered dreams

My words like the waters

Of a cataract

Fall about you

Water the varied forest of your life.

<u>The New Life</u>   February 4, 1983

Life is when you get up in the morning

Pick yourself out of bed and split for work

It's the mistery of crushed expectations

It's counting on

Concentrating on one miserable point

Of view

One lost meaningless statement

That has nothing to do with reality but
becomes reality-work

Now

We have to work to live – but do we have to
live to work?

Right now, I learn

I go to work

My interests are piqued and I am ready to
live

But some people

Work, work, work and they never get a
chance to live

They see nothing outside

They see nothing around

They work during the day and see only dirt,
grit and darkness coming home at night

They have no leisure

They simply are being cheated

Of their right to live

Who is being cheated?

It's similar to sending these people to war

But when these return

There is absolutely nothing

Nothing different

Nothing new

Nothing that can be new

Nothing that can be understood

Total

Complete

Vapidity

<u>Puppet</u>   May 21, 2001

Puppet

Light upon head

Mexican puppet

Dance

Until

The Day of the Dead

Where round all laying

Children are playing

Puppet bows and careers

Shadowed strings

We see these hands

Puppet

<u>The Turtle and the Snake</u>

Good Turtle

Bad Snake

They go

Journey home

Good Turtle finds something not his

Returns it to owner

Bad Snake finds something not his

Sells it

Good Turtle tells the truth

Bad Snake lies

Good Turtle helps a stranger

Bad Snake ignores person in need

They get home

Both are welcome

<u>Yellow Again</u>   October 6, 2001

My wood

Is a yello wood

That is good

Acorns raining down

Like drum beats

All around

Squirrels running

Just

Keeping up

Not taking mind

Of me

While gathering

To dress their tables

In deep, cold winter

The wind

Like a rider

Moves through the trees

Back again

The trees

Bow before their Lady

Raising the color of leaves

In greeting

Sassafras gone yellow

In the evening of the year

Keeps it savory bark

For the interested bite

Sassafras leaves

Tumble down

In acrobatic display

Coming to rest

On the earth

In the middle of the day

Their gentle colored textures

Turned toward the light

Fades into afternoon

Altogether quite bright

Mixing now

Sassafras with maple and elm and oak

Spinning

Spinning down

Like water on a rope

Cascading about me

Carried by the wind

One yellow, one red and another

Yellow again

<u>Tale of Flight</u>   November 6, 1979

See

Little bird

Flitting

On wing

Round, round o'er the corn

O'er the squash

O'er my head

Sky spread

Blue and white

Spinning round the sun

Bird voices

Not flying

Call up to their fellows

Fly on, fly on

Scream

Fly on

Faster and faster flew he too

Over flailing stalks of wheat and corn

The wind with mighty gusts

In a rainless storm

Cobs rattle together

Cacophony uniting

With songs of the birds come flighting

Flying, flying, flying

Gazing
Up

At the sky

Flying, for the sun

Coming closer

And closer

The bird

Flew into

The Sun

A soft wind

Blew o'er the open plain

Lifting, softly

Long hair of the warrier

He tensed

Grasped bow

Hand ever tighter

Eyes closing, halfway

Gaze roving horizon

He turned and ran down the hill

As easy as I stand up

<u>**Telling Tales**</u>   Undated

Ask me
No questions

I will tell you

No lies

If you listen

I will paint

For your ears

Tales you want to hear

I will paint for your eyes

All sorts of colors

In a sweet disguise

<u>Just Stand There</u>   Undated

When your friend

Tells you he's doing heroin

You can read

Black letters in the sky

You see a piece of glass

Flowing in the concrete

Like a feather

You can see that shard

Shatter

You wonder

Does the whirling ocean matter

Think not

Dive in after him

Bring him to the surface

Let them see your face

Let them know you're there

Grab them by the hair

You'll have to

Don't let them go that way

Bring them back and say

I love you

Don't take yourself away

Hold them in your arms

Do not sway

Oh, it'll take all day

And year

But don't give in

To fear

Just stand there

Just stand there

<u>Hail and Farewell</u>   Undated

A lady is getting married today

Here white dress is ready and she is on her
way

A lady is getting married today, today

Everyone is joyful as they gather for the
meeting

While in the church the men are arranging
for the seating

The lady frets and she wonder as she waits
for the car

When it arrives she sees she hasn't got far to
go

Riding in the limo, moving along

When she arrives there they will burst into
song

Walking up the aisle to the man that she
loves

All dressed in grey and she in white gloves

They are happy

Then comes the priest in all his regalia

To join these two together forever

Have you seen a ceremony so long and so
strong?

An ancient remembrance that we've had all
along

Of a life that is peaceful and filled with song

It's a statement of our staying power as it
may be

It makes us more like a flower than we
appear that we are

So, love, love, love

And farewell

May all of your blessings resound like a bell

May your life always be happy, your joy as
deep as a well

And once again I say good-bye

And a hall and farewell

It's a Matter of Time   Undated

It's a matter of time in your heart

I will stay with you forever more

I wake in the morning

Take breakfast on a tray

It seems the next thing

I say goodbye to the day

It's a matter of time in my heart

When will it start?

Don't you think it's time to settle down?

While this old world continues to spin
around

Whirling through each week, each month,
each year

It's a matter of time in my heart

That is driving me on

It's a matter of time

<u>Lace</u>   Undated

Bright morning sun

Waking to the day

Was that a dream?

Was it what is seemed?

The Sun is on the water

Shining on my face

Just a little aside me

Saw that ruffle of lace

<u>Dreams</u>   Undated

Dreams are your life

Dreams are your mind

If you don't know that

You're just living blind

Dreams are your night

Dreams are your day

If you don't know that

There's nothing to say

<u>Memory</u>   Undated

Working

Today

An odd sensation

Your memory

So real

Perfect my recollection

Until the ringing metal before me

Brings me back from you

Whenever my mind in wandering

It most of the time meets you

How is it that pain chases love

Like a hawk does the dove?

Within my arms embraced

Memory

<u>Miss You</u>　　　　　Undated

When I dream of you

When you enter my life

All good things around you

All things clear of strife

Pained the memory

Of beauty once glanced

How fragile the imagery

Linked in romance

<u>Enough For You</u>   Undated

On the ancient morning

I arose

First thought

Of you

In repose

In wooded glen

Across windswept field

Ponder I

The memory of your brow

Silken skin

Hair like golden gossamer

Frames your face

Love

Longing for you

This journey's end to return

I remember you for me

My remembrance

I hope

Enough for you

<u>Looking For You</u>   Undated

Walking

In the night

Through grass and whispers

Across the brook

Through the wood

A field and some odd smoke

Remember I those days and nothing less, nor
more

Ragged leaves

Bundled by the wind

Whirlstorms at my feet

Smile on your face

Like warm sunlight spilling

On cold October day

Then, in new New Town living

Crossing whatever wide boulevard there

Boots crunching

You, looking for love

I, looking for you

<u>**Since Then**</u>   Undated

What

Could you be doing

Without me

No longer a care

Hoping for more

Expecting nothing

How perfection slipped

Through my fingers

While remaining

Carefully perched

Tell me

Will I know?

I know you for all times

Out of sight but never out of mind

My soul, one half, waiting

Tell me

I will not always hear

This silence

Unless we two

Together

Are alone

Where have you gone

Since then?

More Than a Friend   Undated

Too close

Perhaps

This blood to yours

Parallel courses

Joined

At junction

Then life tied

Together

My arms are spread

You are welcome to them

May we never part

Ring the bell and cast the flower petals

Your feet upon the floor

Like bells to me

My heart rebounds

Your return

To me

More than a friend

<u>**Never Let You Go**</u>   Undated

I told you

And I told you so

I told you so

Life is a dream

To be dreamed

By the dreamer

I told you why

And I told you why too

Our lives

Just beginning

Each day

New

No matter

How many

Years pass

I have waited for ages

Beside the stars

I thought it a dream

I had so long ago

That I would find you here

Never let you go

What Will I Be?   Undated

Where are you going?

Where

Have you gone?

What troubled you?

Let me hear it from your lips

The words that will freeze me

Transform me

Set me free

If need be

Tell me true then

Without the truth

What will I be?

<u>**You See**</u>   Undated

The sky was blue there

The sky is blue here

The sky was blue then

The sky is blue now

Time passed quickly then

Time passes quickly now

Turning round

Turning round again

Where do you hope to be?

The beginning is the end

You see

<u>**The Legend of the Three Arrows**</u>

As I recall it told to me – by Alfred Brock

Mori Motonari was a very powerful man in Japan. He was a great warrior and many samurai were loyal to him.

Though his province was small he was able to overcome and conquer much larger enemies to the east and the west.

He was an honorable and just leader to his people

.

Three of his sons rose to the rank of General in the army of the Mori clan. They were called Mōri Takamoto, Kikkawa Motoharu, and Kobayakawa Takakage.

He encouraged them to work together for the good of the Mori clan.

Being wise Mori Motonari knew that one day these three strong leaders may come to blows and all their hard work be torn asunder.

He called them to a dinner where they engaged in dining and entertainment.

 When the evening was in full bloom Mori Motonari called a stop to it and summoned the three Generals before him.

 They came forward in respect and sat before him on tatami mats. Their weapons, sharp and ready at their sides.

 Each one in succession Mori Motonari called forward to him. To each one in succession he gave them a thickly formed arrow and asked them to break it.

Each one in succession easily broke arrow given to them. Hardly hiding their contempt they returned to their seats on their tatami mat.

Mori Motonari called for the broken arrows to be removed from before him. In the silence the sound of a sweeping broom could be heard out into the garden beyond.

While his kind servant and Captain swept away the splinters of the arrows Mori Motonari reached behind him and drew out three more arrows just as thick and strong as the ones that had been broken before him. As his Captain swept Mori Motonari tied the arrows together with aged but powerful hands. His fingers carefully tied ceremonial knots in the cords he used to combine the three arrows. All gathered looked on with interest and curiousity

With the floor clean between them Mori
Motonari again asked each of the Generals
in turn to come forward and break the new
bundle of arrows.

 Each of them tried and each of them failed
to break the bundle.

 'So it is,'said Mori Motonari to his sons and
Generals, 'that individually each of these
arrows may be broken easily but tied
together, and joined thus, their strength is
greater and so they cannot be broken.''

The dinner then began again and continued
long into the night. It was a fine evening.

<u>Today the Clouds Arrayed</u>

Today the clouds arrayed
In circular display
crown of white
Upon the bright
Greens erupt
from earth
stepping of life moves
forward again

<u>Trace the New Tattoo</u>
2021

She considers a new Tattoo

A reclining goddess

Spinning a world on her finger

Gazing upon her I ask

May I trace the new tattoo?

She cautiously does acquiesce

Reclines herself

Upon the deeply cushioned

Red, crushed velvet divan

Gestures with her hand

Lays her head to rest

Watching me closely

One finger extended

The tip only

Gently touches her skin

Smooth and soft like sea foam

Colored white

Like untouched snows on mountaintops

My finger alights upon her leg

Just to the side of her right knee

Formed like a powdered dome on the
steppes

Her leg flowing out from my touch

Cream colored and shaded

Like the sands of the desert

Her legs stretch into infinity

I groan lowly

Draw in my breath

Remember where I am

My finger moves lightly

Along her shin to ankle

The gentle rise rushing down

To her crystal foot and toes

My finger

Seeking where the new tattoo

Should go

I briefly and without thought

Envy the intimacy of the tattoo artist

So closely entwined

For such a short period

With this woman before me

Bound with pain and blood

Through an ordeal

She sometimes prefers

To conversation

Catching myself again

My finger runs along her toes

To under them

Knowing full well

No tattoo of this kind can go there

Sensing my change of mood

She adjusts herself

Looking down at me

The clouds outside the window

Change position

My finger continues its traverse

Along the sole of her foot

She smiles and shakes her head

Gently

My finger moves on to her heel

The underpart of her ankle

To her shin and outer thigh

Moving along the outside

Of her hip

I pause in my mind

My soul vibrating

Like a strong chord struck

On to the curve of her side

Lightly brushing through

The blousy white material

Draped upon her body

Her white blouse

Trimmed with light blue

Up to the inner part of her arm

To her shoulder

Down, down, down

Tracing her rounded biceps

Her taught triceps

To her elbow

Her lower arm

Wrist

Hand

Back up again

To her shoulder

Wavering there

As I look into her eyes

Swimming deeply in those watery worlds

Falling off my own spinning globe

Suspended in space and time

Across her upper shoulder

To her neck

Ear

Tracing round

To the back of her head

To the hairline

Where alabaster skin

Gives way to golden hair

The hairline

Of find down

My finger lingers

Passing back to her cheek

I touch her lips

Look down

Place my hand on hers

Lay my head in her lap

Tracing her tattoo in my mind

Across my heart

www.ingramcontent.com/pod-product-compliance
Lightning Source LLC
Chambersburg PA
CBHW061530120726
48001CB00004B/1470